I0669517

Maria was born in Sao Paulo, Brazil, in 1931. Ever since she was a child, she always found a pencil, handy. She was very passionate about drawing and writing, and still is. Doing painting was her main activity but writing was always present. Creativity and imagination were the reasons behind this book, thinking about her grandchildren and great-grandchildren. She has also published two books in Portuguese: *Atlantis: Atol de Formigas*, 2006; and *0 Rei das Orquideas,* 2012. Both the books can be found on Amazon.

A Drop of Water

Maria Anna Machado

AUSTIN MACAULEY PUBLISHERS™
LONDON • CAMBRIDGE • NEW YORK • SHARJAH

Ordering Information:
Quantity sales: special discounts are available on quantity purchases by corporations, associations, and others. For details, contact the publisher at the address below.

Anna Machado, Maria
A Drop of Water

ISBN 9781641823654 (Paperback)
ISBN 9781641823661 (Hardback)
ISBN 9781641823678 (E-Book)

The main category of the book — Adventure

www.austinmacauley.com/us
First Published (2018)
Austin Macauley Publishers LLC
40 Wall Street, 28th Floor
New York, NY 10005
USA

mail-usa@austinmacauley.com
+1 (646) 5125767

To all my family, my four children, my nine grandchildren, and eight great-grandchildren.

A Drop of Water

She was found alive in the yam leaf. The mild wind shook the leaf, causing her to shake, and the sun made her look like a liquid diamond.

She was happy!

Having to leave her soft spot due to the hot sun, the water drop took advantage of a sudden gust and said goodbye to the leaf, rolling down the trunk.

WOW!

When it got to the ground, it saw a small stream of water and it joined in with the other drops.

They sang down the streets.

Hi...

Along the way, they found a dark hole and
entered through it.
They stayed still until they saw the sun again.

WOW...

Quietly, the water drop went along with the others to a small river that meanders behind a village...

It was observing everything around.

Oh... the sun!

A girl with a glass collected a portion of water and, along with the other drops, were taken to a shack.
The glass was placed on a rustic table and a yellow flower joined them.

Hi...

Sometimes later, a man came by and threw the cup away. His hoarse voice was vibrating in the air:
"We do not have enough cups for this nonsense."

The poor little yellow flower was laying on the grass.

Oops...

But the drop of water was more alive than ever,
holding onto the grass until a harsh movement
shook the grass and lifted up again.
It was a bird passing by and took
the grass.
It wasn't afraid.

Oh!

They went very high and weren't afraid.

They went up very high but it was not afraid at all!
"Your mother, the cloud, lives even higher."

WOW...

When they arrived at the bird's nest, the grass was entangled along others. The water drop was infiltrated within the twigs and started falling until it hit the ground.

There, it got comfortable on a rock and observed the new space...

Bye...

The moment's peace did not last long, as a deafening sound took over.
It was coming from a chainsaw that was chopping the tree down with its bird's nest.

There was no time to complain.

Oh!

It was captured with a bunch of soil by the bulldozer and was thrown in a man-made lake.

Wow...

The drop was shaken off like a wet dog and got with the others. After a little while, something else began to happen...

They started turning green and were having a hard time breathing.

After lots of struggles, the drop was able to grab onto a green bottle that slowly floated by in the middle of all the pollution.

Finally, the bottle came to a stop by a bunch of debris.

Come...

A homeless person retrieved the bottle for recycling. The drop inside the bottle was dreaming...

"Oh! Sea, my father, if I could return to you, I would never leave again."

Oh!

Sometime later, it heard the sound of a train. It was a dream to think that it could travel the world alone.

After the uncomfortable silence, it felt lost...

Sometime after, the bottle was taken from the bag and shaken violently to get rid of the dirt.

Then it hit the sand.

Bye...

While still somewhat faint due to being frightened, it felt comforted by the cool foamy water of its father, the ocean, who generously took it in without asking for any explanations.

Home sweet home!

Home sweet home!

The End